Visit the Vet

Written by Suzy Senior

Illustrated by Michael Emmerson

Collins

This is Fuzz.

She is sick.

Shaz puts Fuzz into a box.

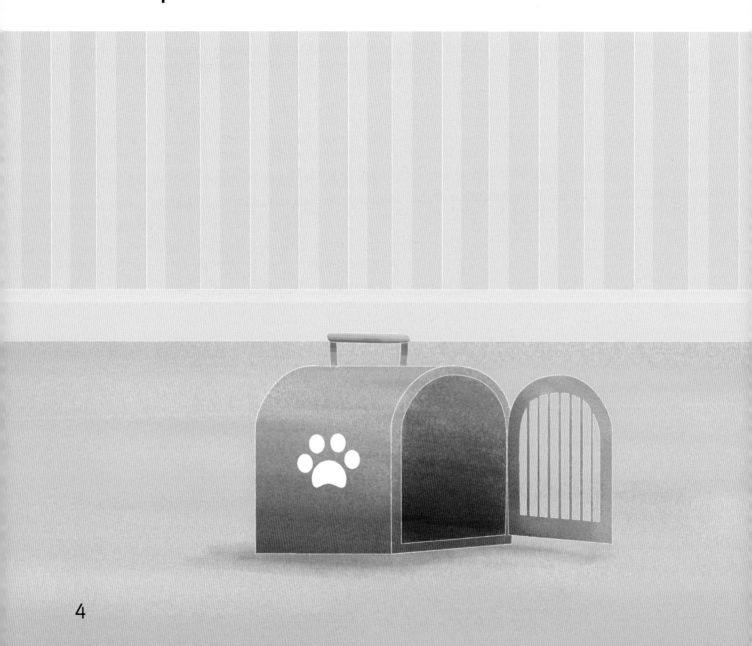

They rush off to the vet.

The vet pats Fuzz and checks her.

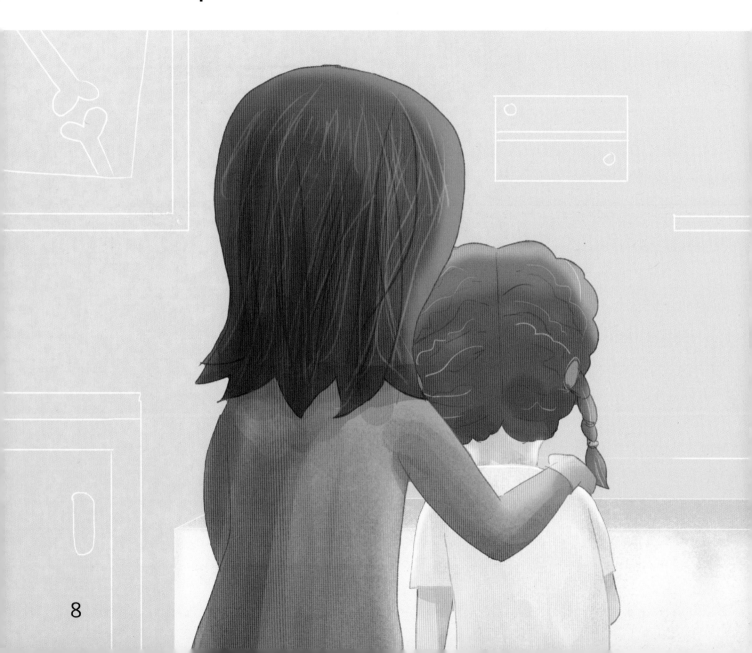

Fuzz has tablets.

She will get well.

Shaz thanks the vet.

Off they go!

/sh/

14

ZZ

After reading

Letters and Sounds: Phase 3

Word count: 39

Focus phonemes: /v/ /w/ /x/ /z/ zz /ch/ /sh/ /th/ /nk/

Common exception words: she, the, they, go, puts, into, to, and, her

Curriculum links: Understanding the world

Early learning goals: Reading: read and understand simple sentences; use phonic knowledge to decode regular words and read them aloud accurately; read some common irregular words

Developing fluency

- Your child may enjoy hearing you read the book.
- Encourage your child to read the sentences with expression. Check they notice the exclamation mark at the end of the story and read this sentence with extra expression to emphasise the happy ending.

Phonic practice

- On page 8, focus on **checks**. Ask your child to find the two pairs of letters that each make one sound. (/ch/ and ck)
- Ask your child to find the two letters that make one sound in each of these words before reading them:

  Shaz   Fuzz   off   well   she

- On page 12, point to **thanks** and ask your child which pairs of letters make one sound before asking them to read the sentence. (th/a/nk/s)
- Look at the "I spy sounds" pages (14–15) together. Point to the shoes and say "shoes", emphasising the /sh/ sound. Point to the drink and say "fizzy", emphasising the "zz" sound. Challenge your child to find more words containing these sounds. Explain that the sound can be at the beginning, middle or end of the words, too. (e.g. *ship*, *shell*, *shapes*, *cushion*, *fish*; *Fuzz*, *buzz*, *fizz*, *puzzle*)

Extending vocabulary

- Talk to the children about the meaning of opposites. Discuss what words are the opposite to these:

  she (*he*)   her (*him*)   will (*won't*)   is (*isn't*)   into (*out of*)   has (*hasn't*)